INTRODUCTION

This is a collection of poems from the age of 5 to 50, organized into three parts, the title of the book, Crushed Green Ice, being the name of the first part. The second being Tokyo Wakes Up and the third, The Energy of Concrete Dreams. They are roughly chronological. The first volume contains earlier poems and the middle volume later poems and the third volume the most recent.

The poems are there to entertain, awaken and shock the reader. They will hopefully leave the person with something to think about.

We are living in an ever changing world where it seems that we have to move faster in order to catch up. These poems reflect that ever changing reality. As we change -reality changes. Our subjective experiences loom large in our youth and we often forget that there are other ways of seeing things. Maybe you can see something of yourself here, of the times, of the person in the poem, who is inside looking out. Maybe the perspectives you see here are like or very different from your own.

The poet has tried not to lose touch with a sense of humanity and purpose in these poems, be it an observation of nature, a social critique or a humorous analysis. There are often strong feelings and opinions expressed, to the extent the reader may say to themselves: I don't like that at all or I really can identify with that. Whatever your opinion, if it makes you think and feel strongly, one way or another, then it has served its purpose.

In compiling this collection, the poet is bringing together the writings of half a lifetime; some previously published in collections or small magazines, some jotted in biro in notebooks, when out and about, some typed hastily on a computer.

The poet has chosen those she feels are of sufficient interest to be read and hopes the reader will enjoy what is on offer.

It is not easy to be a poet and certainly not easy to get published. The poet hopes that this collection is not an ego trip but that the fun of doing it and hopefully entertaining a few readers should make it a worthwhile venture.

Happy reading!

CRUSHED GREEN ICE

A

Collection of Poems from

5 to 50

By

Felicity Diane Kaye

Published in 2009 by YouWriteOn.com

First Edition

Published by YouWriteOn.com

Now we are alone

Spring of 76……………

Now we are alone
Everyone is gone
Now we are alone
I, and my consciousness
Now we are thinking, together,
In unison
Of the past, the present
And the future
Now we are considering time
Now we are waiting for peace

Now we are alone
There is much time to plan
To formulate truth
To explore ideas
Now we are alone
There is time to wait

Now we are alone
I am listening to the silence
To the hissing of the gas fire
Which emphasizes my aloneness
Now we are alone
Now we are truly alone
We are truly alone

Poetry For Two

Poetry to soothe your spirit
Poetry to calm you
Poetry to make you feel good

Poetry to quieten you
To humour you
To frighten you

Poetry to soothe you
To smooth you
To tell the truth -
To you
I would give all my poetry
To you I would write verses
Simple and pure
If you would only
Love me true

The Gypsy Caravan

There is a little caravan in town
It's always there when I'm around
Gay colours, painted red and green
It's not for sale, but it's my dream

If ever I should run away
Which I seem to do most every day
I'd take that caravan with me
And camp in green fields by the sea

With shady woods in my domain
I'd shelter there in the rain
I'd never be alone out there
Not with the birds singing in the air

I'd sit and dream, make daisy chains
And count my losses not my gains
I'd always pick a rose in June
And weave fantasies beneath the moon

I'd hope that happiness would come
When I'm all alone and in the sun
I'd try and consider each new day
Knowing that I was always free
And live with nature in harmony

Curtains

Summer of 76……………..

Gold leaves on a varied cloth
Rich and tinselly, especially
Where the arc of light
Caught them.
Patterns.
Rows of leaves holding hands.
Joined in Royal Ecstasy.
Bright gold sheen
And darker shadows. Stripes of cloth
Rippled in sculptured undulations.
Streaks of shadow.
Creases and crepes of cloth.
Filigree leaves. Heraldic swirls in pale gold,
White embroidery.
Relief ornamentation of pattern
And pleat.

Eureka

Eureka
Euterpe
In everything you do
Ernest
In Earnest!

But
When you paint
U reek a
Of
Terps!

Eeeeeeeeeee

Ice-plant feel cold
Egg-plant feel old
Eglantine time for mine
Ergo eons too late.

Softly…..

There was a soft sultana
Sitting in the sun
Contemplating a bashful banana
That she fancied.
Said sultana to banana
I come from Santana.
I'd like a Rum Baba
Said the banana.

Hull

By day…..

In bloody Hull,
Down 'umberside
Where fish stinks in the air,

Where mucky river flows through docks
And all the people stare
If you wear funny clothes.

In bloody Hull,
Where town is full
Of gangs and dockers and dustmen
Of blue jeans, toughies and soap factory ladies;

There's not a place that's greyer
Than ever a place could be
On a wet Monday morning.

Hull

By night.....

This is really a city!
Cats in the alley ways at night
Where the fish and chip papers accumulate.

And the casino club on Spring Bank
Where it's all happening
And the big-time gamblers in winkle-pickers lose their money
And the croupiers lose their knickers, that's not funny.
The rich tried to make it quick, but they lost their wits
At the Mayfair.

In the Mecca ballroom you can dance 'til you drop
From the hits of the '60s to 70's pop.

In the fog,

The cars make faces at each other
Where they screech to a halt at the crossroads
Receiving only
The white, steely glare from the neon street lamps.

From the river,
Comes the foghorn symphony in B flat major.
The owl's solitary solo echoes in the air
As if to disturb the sleeping birds,
Whose chirpy sounds could provide percussion.
And the yakety-yak of the alley cats
Sounds like violins
And when they jump on the dustbins
The lids rattle

Like cymbals.

<u>Even the Wimpy Bar's shut</u>
You want to escape..............

Though the Wimpy Bar is shut
And you know you're in a rut
Don't allow yourself to give way to despair.

Though the cinema is showing
Only X films, and your knowing conscience
Tells you that
It's Holy Day.

Though the mud that's in the river
Down by the docks looks ever thinker,
Don't take that final plunge
Into the depths.

Though the buses are not frequent,
Please don't become delinquent
And start to kick about
Old tins of things.

Just stop a while and ponder
Of the town
You'll grow 'er fonder
When its fishy air
You'll leave far, far behind.

Though it's raining, bloody raining,
And your feet and face are waning.
Your frustration it is mounting
As the hours you are counting
'Til back to dear old London you will go.

But…But… Don't despair

There is a church that's open
Where you can swear to God
You won't come here again, Amen.

7 O'clock - Morning in September

(Written in garden of the Avenue's house I grew up in, in Hull)

Leaves - sun shaded, sun-faded
Leaves, curled twisted
Laurels evergreen
Caesar's wreath, broken, thrown into the fire-heap
Twisted
Dust, ash blue, grey white, black
Dust to dust
White dove on the telegraph pole
Grey-inflated chest and cooing
Neck strong - bulging
Mint sweet-smelling purple flowered
Hinting at Spring
Freshness amongst the dead
Apples - hewn by worms and
Wormed by wasps
Holes - last orifices of summer
Holes, holes in the earth
Convolvulus, creeping, strangled
Gasping for juice
White poisoned flowers amongst the shadows
The arrows point to the ground
The tubers dig into the earth
Strangling
Conflict between
Conflict between?
Impulsiveness and self-will
The morning begins
The fog-horn from the river
Swelled with officialdom blows

To his calls answers the wind
Battling the leaves
Slashing the trees
Disturbing the birds
A money spider runs across the walk under my feet
Halts or so I imagine
When I stare at it
Then scrambles by and hides itself
Gone
Disappeared into the brick
The morning begins

Ode to a Muddy River

Thursday morning; and the muddy river
Slides its oily tails under the bridge, laps
At the barges and the tugs, collects flakes
Of paint and tears the liverwort from the banks
Where it clings in lime-green agony.

Slobbers like a pitiful, never-ending tongue
Forever thirsty and forever seeking.
It gulps down quantities of rain
And inflates itself, smoothing down
The caked mud at its sides.

It rises a little with the pomposity
Of an over anxious crawler.
The river knows its sins
The river knows its nothing but
A cess-pool for rust and rats

For crusts, drowned cats.
For wooden planks, for putrid tanks;
Where mattresses and old sofas
Rot together
In decaying harmony.

The river knows its sins
It knows is limits.
It knows its slime beneath your feet.
It thank the post office clerk for fishing
There on Sundays
But whether he ever catches any fish, is doubtful.

(Dedicated to the river Hull)

Memories of Brittany................? (Sort of)

I think a pickled mouse is something you should try.
Though you'll find it hard to obtain one
That's pickled in wine vinegar with rye.
But that's beside the point, 'cos mostly they are pickled
In vodka and lime. A flavour sublime -
To savour the palate and tickle the wallet.
A delicacy s rare from Africa;
Rarer than the rarest caviar.
Posher than the poshest Amoricaine Oyster,
That are cultivated in Brittany,
Around Locmariquer.

To be eaten with care
The rarest of rare.
Spin out the chew,
Now I'm just telling you
For your own good;
'Cos a mouse's sinew
Ain't half hard to chew -
It's like chewing wood.
But I'm making the suggestion
If you're prone to indigestion
On how to avoid congestion in your works.

In other words to stop
The hiccups and the burps.

But on the whole I think
A pickled mouse with pink champagne,
Is all one needs in order to regain
A sense of à la carte
A sense of the art of eating,
Into one's daily répas.

(A sort of poetic concoction remembering the oysters I used to eat in Brittany as a child, where we spent a lot of summer holidays)

<u>**St Mary's School Field, Hull**</u>

Girls lie on the long green grass
Under the hot, summer sun.
The heat lies thick and stifling on their faces.
Amongst the grass lurk spiders and flies and
Amongst the sweet-smelling, yellow hay
That the big machine only yesterday has mown up
And left in rows to dry in the hot sun.

The sunlight plays upon the grass,
Reflected in the yellow, enamel buttercups
That if crushed, the thin shiny film
Peels of the petals like paint;
Upon the rouge-tipped daisies
And clover
And lemon-yellow dandelions
With their, jagged, bitter leaves.

It plays among the May blossom.
Sweet, white and sticky,
Hanging in loose, fragrant blossoms

From black, thorny boughs.
The May that they pick
To lay before some chipped plaster statue
Of Virgin Mary, in the classroom,
Where the sun shines through dusty windows and flickers
Lightly amongst the blossoms
And the cool, green leaves
And on the varnished wood of the shelf.

Soon the girls will come in
When the bell echoes from the school
Disturbing the thick afternoon heat.
They will rise
Shaking grass out their hair
And smoothing crumpled skirts
Screwing their faces up
Against the sharp sunlight
And return slowly
Relaxed and whispering
To sit in the stuffy classroom
Where the air is scarce and study
Whilst the afternoon
Goes on its own way
Outside in the busy town.

Autumn

It's Autumn now.
The leaves are brown.
A child's delight I have.
The skies are grey.
The wind blows.
See me run!
Catch a falling leaf in your hand
Then let it go
See where it falls
Look a conker

Look a fallen dream
When we were young....
See the children in the pyres of golden leaves
Alsatian dogs
Their coats ruffled by the breeze
An old woman's dulled eye as she glances
Sweet, short glances
Then she passes on by...
Does it make her cry?
She permit's a sigh
Then passes on by.
For her it's not just Autumn..
But the Autumn of her life.

<u>Autumn</u>

A field full of golden corn
Rolling over
To the horizon
Where fir trees
Gather on the hill
Peeping over the top
Like scrubbing bushes

A wood full of
Brambles and weeds
Each leaf
And strand of grass
Covered in rain

Many people
Walking and talking
Chewing ears of corn
Meditating
On something beautiful
In nature

One single poppy

Small and wilting
One dot of red colour
Amongst the yellow corn
The opium of the poet's spirit

A Great Respect for Worms

Don't you look down on worms!
Squash me!
I have a great respect for worms,
We say: 'You worm, you make me squirm!
You're lower than the low.'
But worms make flowers grow!
They dig right down,
Dragging the debris of leaves with them.
Munching, crunching,
Squirming, turning their way,
Through mud,
Out of mud,
Grows Solomon's Seal,
And lilies.
Out of mud, grows wisdom.
When you're in the mud,
You have to get out
Only a worm can tell you how!

(Previously published in Changing Seasons, Poetry Today, 1998)

Weeds

Weeds are the proletariat of the flowers
Always causing trouble
Growing where threshold's
Overrunning ordered existence
These multitudinous brats

Strangling
The pure rose of thought

The weeds are on strike
They are not refusing to grow
Or to go to work on the lilies
But they are having a grow-in, grow-out, grow-up
As a protest
They are overrunning order
In my inner garden

Weeds are not devils
They merely unpaved the way
For the devils to climb in
Through the crazy-paving

Imps lurk in the dark recesses of my heart
Like imps in the corners
Of the paving stones

<u>Harvest Festival, West Yorks</u>

A strange site met my eyes
As I entered the local church.
The door swung open, the
Stone walls comforted me. Inside

Where fruits of the autumn, fruits
Of the crimson-ochre fall
Arrayed around the church.
Tomatoes with a foolish grin

On oak. Oranges with
A dimple in their chin. A cabbage
In a cryptic corner. Vaguely

Green on wooden sheen.
Bananas, fresh and pointing up
To heaven. A brass eagle surveyed
The church with gleaming eyes.

A bunch of grapes adorned his neck,
Gleamed like wax, yet were real.
Gold and white silk tassels
Like a priest's robe covered his breast.

A ridiculous, yet arrogant
Bird; about to 'prey' upon
His congregation.
Eagerly surveying the now

Empty pews. Six eggs on
The piano. More fruit in a
Basket. And to top it all.
A tin of mushroom soup!

Does God like tinned soup,
I wonder. If so, has he a tin
Opener around?
If I had a guest I wanted

To honour, I would not
Leave him a tin of soup and say
'There, help yourself; self-
Catering around here, you know'. Yet

When the service begins
And the higher notes of the hymns
Rattle the piano
Which rattles the tin. Who would be

God then? The harvest loaf
Is moulded out of burnished dough
Into sheaves of corn.

Slightly nibbled it looks. Not by

The harvest mouse that's shaped
From the bread, with a wiggly
Tail and a currant for
Its eye. The church is a country

Kitchen. The carpeted
Aisle. The knitted floor cushions. The
Copper plates, the candles
And the flower arrangements.

Chrysanthemums, holly
Poisonous red berries, creepers;
The ivy all laid out
Beneath the windows, in baskets

On ledges, at the side
Of pews. The font packed full of flowers
The church has a somewhat
pagan air, dedicated to

Honour Pan, the God
Of nature; not the God we know.
Left of the altar
A winding staircase leads up to

The tower where the bells chime, bells
Like bluebell notes. Fairy music.
A fern frond brushes my
Side, as I walk out of the church.

The door swings to. The world
Is regained. The sun blesses me.

Mathematical Attractions

Oh, I love the Professor
P + Q =
Me and You
Penelope and Quentin
But are my pigtails offendin' you?
Your equation's
Our liaison
A téte a téte
Let's fix a date
At 8
Your number
X's mine means
We're =
At the top of the triangle

It's mathematical attractions
It's mathematical attractions
Your equation's our liaison
Your equation's our liaison
And we don't need no deductions
No we don't need no deductions
From mathematical attractions
It's mathematical attractions

But you have the power
You're an entire oligarchy
Just for me.
I don't know the right angle to take
But I'm 90% hot
Don't you think we can equate our lot?
About the diameter of a circle
I'm not certain
But it's only noon now
At night your circle is my moon

Your *s are shooting stars to me

The gold stars symbolic of our future unity
123 perhaps
456
Betwixt the two of us
6 prodigies to please
Let's just leave it to the B's + the B's

It's mathematical attractions
It's mathematical attractions
Your equation's our liaison
Your equation's our liaison
And we don't need no deductions
No we don't need no deductions
From mathematical attractions
It's mathematical attractions

(I might as well dedicate this to the teacher who enabled me to get 70% one year(way above the usual 23%) for maths while at Grammar School, although I don't think he , luckily, ever knew of my feelings! The symbols and numbers are meant to be read as their names)

The Angry Child Inside

The angry child inside,
Needs to be reconciled with the adult you.
You can never forget about injustices,
At the age of two.
But you can make an agreement
To accept the angry child inside.

We all have an angry boy,
An angry girl.
Who could never speak out,
But now we are adult
We should use that
Anger to better our life,
Not poison it.

Use your anger,
To create something positive,
Something good.
Use it to sing a song,
Write a poem,
Undo an injustice;
Help your fellow men.
Us it for change,
As food for thought, for action.

I've got an angry child inside.
It wants to get out, to scream and shout,
To let it all hang out!

(Previously published in Family Ties, Poetry Today, 2001)

Jubilee, June '77

(written while in London during that time)

Around St Pauls
The crowds thickened
Children peeped through the railings
We waited two hours
To see the Queen in pink
American accents echoed
"We wanna see the Queen, the Queen!'
She waved, smiled and disappeared
Some people had even brought
Their own ladders
From which they could wave
Union jack flags

Then the rush to the underground
The crowds of pushing people
Going into the tunnel
It reminded me of something I'd read about the war

When people were killed as they ran underground
To escape the bombings

Then back in Yorkshire
I got on a Silver Jubilee bus to Leeds
Absolutely painted silver
I felt honoured getting on at the bus station
The graffiti on the walls proclaimed:
'Down with the Jubilee,
Long live Socialism!'
It could be down with you or me next, I thought.
The thunder in the sky rumbled
The lightening struck
I wondered whether Amin
Would really turn up at the Commonwealth conference.

Time Out had publicized
Hardly any Jubilee celebrations at all
I reflected
Just the details of her salary
Was The Queen justified in getting all that money, I thought,
As I watched a man clean up the streets?
But then, where would be without the Royals' worldwide diplomacy.

The next morning
The Jubilee was still with me
Union Jack flags in the greengrocer's window
Red, white and blue streamers
And my silver milk bottle top
Had Jubilee stamped all over it.

There is No Alternative.

There is no alternative
To our situation.
She spoke as the self-appointed dictator

Of the new monetarist economy.
There is no alternative
She said, as she rearranged her cabinet
With a few young studs.
There is no alternative
As the last hunger striker died
And the one after gave up.
No alternative as the British soldier shot another
Child by mistake, with a plastic bullet.
No alternative
As he himself, was later killed in the Falklands.
No alternative
She said, as the 18 year old unemployed youth
Went to the detention centre for 3 months
For throwing an egg in her face.
No alternative
Said the police, as the Bradford 12 were refused bail.
No alternative
As the radical paper seller was arrested
For peddling without a licence
In the street.
We have no choice
No alternative
But to stay in NATO
The Russians are waiting to invade us
From behind the Iron curtain.
No alternative, she said
But to let Everyone invest in us
Let us invest in the third world.
No alternative
Agreed the shareholders, senators and bankers
But to invest.
No alternative
She said, as the police brought out the rubber bullets,
CS gas and machine guns during the miners' strike.
No alternative
As the latest black prisoner
Driven paranoid by the system

Died in police hands.
She had
No alternative
But to abstain from condemning
South Africa's incursion into Angola
Where thousands of brave ANC fighters
Died for nothing

But the people screamed;
We have an alternative
We present it to you
In short; anarchy,
If you don't listen to us;
There will be an eruption.
Because there was no alternative to the poll tax
School children took to the streets in gangs
Smashed the shop windows
And threw bottles at police vans.

How much hate is contained
Or can be contained in these words:
'There is no alternative'.

Item (early 1980's)

I travel for my pleasure
Because where I am
Nobody wants me
My family don't want me
I feel I am a mistake,
And my brother thinks I'm a problem,
'Cos I'm not logical enough
And I make silly remarks over the table
When I go to visit him
'Not you again,' he says,
Then disappears upstairs.

They all keep waiting for me
To go lunatic
They are always discussing
How near I am to it.

My street doesn't want me.
They don't like my anarchist songs
Which I play on my guitar
Strings in D minor,
A discordant chord.
On a summer's day,
I hear them muttering
Through the open window,
'I wish she'd go away!'
(But I'm only a poet).

I've just moved.
My suburb doesn't want me.
They glare at me in Woolworths
In Wood Green,
Where I do my shopping.
People's eyes accuse me
Of starting a riot
(But I only write poetry,
I didn't try it out in actuality.)
Even the Writer's group don't want me
They didn't understand my poem; one said,
'First she insults the Irish,
Then she insults the blacks!'
It was supposed to be a poem about inequality,
But they missed the point.

'You've got too many ideas, my girl!'
My mother used to say
I knew she wanted a daughter
Who could cook and pray.
'Please stop asking me all those
Endless questions!'

She used to say.
'Or I'll have to send you away,
I can't cope for another day!
You're giving me indigestion.'

Now my landlord doesn't want me.
He's Scottish,
And his brother has a pub in South Africa.
He told me not to speak to the Africans next door.
I told them their sunflowers were great.
Now he wants me to emigrate, too!
We all have different views

My jobs have never wanted me
I can tell you that
For a fact!
35 words per minute
Was always too slow,
And I was always 15 minutes late,
So they asked me to go

My boss didn't like me wearing trousers,
Or reading books about 'bra burners',
In my lunch hour
But I wasn't one really, you know.
And the coffee I made for him
Always had too much or too little sugar in it.
Or I put milk in the wrong cups,
Or mixed up the mugs
They asked me to make sandwiches for lunch,
But they threw them in the bin,
Because my fillings wouldn't stay in.
Then they'd say:
'You can't make sandwiches like Lynn,
Can you please go away!'

I tried to be a teacher,
But my supervisor said

I wasn't quite on the ball,
And I'd better pull my socks up
Or I might fall
Down
He said my teaching schemes were a bit near the bone,
I wasn't getting through
And they had a Marxist tone.
But I hadn't read a sentence of 'Das Capital',
I forgot the students' names,
(All of them looked threateningly the same)
Then I told the Headmaster
I liked the idea of steel bands in Wakefield High
He looked me severely in the eye
And said 'Brass bands are what we like round here!'
I spoke up for 'Socialist Weekly' being freely distributed
In the staffroom,
As copies kept disappearing from tables
I didn't put them there,
I was only speaking up in
The interests of democracy.
The other staff wouldn't talk to me
They whispered about me in corners, saying:
'She'll get her due, she's a lefty too!'
I don't know what upset them, do you?

So, I travel for my pleasure.
Hoping for some chance encounter
In a strange land.
Pretending I'm a politician
Or a spy,
Or an envoy with a mission
Of love.

A Blank Wall

Sometimes I think
I do not think at all.
I am not good at thinking
Neither am I good at staring blankly at the wall,
Though I often do it.
Sitting thinking about thinking
Of actions to be made,
Bills to be paid.
Realities to be remade.
Dreaming of dreaming of dreaming.
Suspended actions in space
And flashbacks to a different place.
Déjà vu haunts me,
As does ennui too,
It taunts me.
Do something, create, act, react
But don't just sit back
And think about thinking while
Dreaming of dreaming about dreaming.

Sometimes I know
I will not do at all.
I see my face in a mirror
And wish it was a brick wall.
Often I do nothing at all,
But sleep and read, how
Appalling it is to be such a bore.
Knowing I always want more and more.
If I could write or if I could paint
Everything would be fine,
And tomorrow could wait.
But I'm not a star
Just a solitary bar
In the chords of life
And just
Someone's wife.

Finsbury Park, London..................

Silence in the Night

Silence in the night
The owl cries
The town sighs
And the cars mumble
The wind ruffles the leaves

Silence in the night
Spring sleeps in the corners
The cold, fresh air
Breaths of winter

Silence in the night
The white moonlight peeps
Through the open window
Or glows with green candour
Behind the mossy velvet curtains
In my bedroom

Silence in the night
The tube threads its way
Through myriad tunnels
And bumbles its way
Into the red-bricked suburbs
Churning out noise in the sooty,
Newspapered, greasy, aroma'd, damp,
Clinging night air
Under a back-street sky
Scarred with a lucid, pink afterglow
Reminiscent of fairs and a faked orient

Silence in the night
And who's to say there is no silence?
When the mystery of slumber
Unfolds in the night

And weaves its way
Among the town and countryside.
The night speaks for itself.

Evolution or Revolution?

If there's going to be a division in this world
Is it to be revolution or evolution?
It's hard to make a decision
With precision
Unless one has a vision
And what solution is there to pollution?
In our nation
The situation of inflation
Cannot be solved without devotion
And no commotion
But one thinks with emotion of malnutrition
Yet we are all in need of tuition
To teach is to ration out our passion
Get ourselves in locomotion
And stop watching television
To work with more devotion
To come to a solution
So that we feel no retribution
'Cos we're not acting with decision
For a new world revolution
Yes, can we ration out our passion?
Can we ration out our passion?
Can we ration out our passion?

The world can’t set you free

No the world can’t set you free
We’re a corrupt society
And we’re losing out on liberty

Only much faster
Heading for disaster
As you walk beneath the neon lights
Of the city whose very heights
Gave you your birthright

Walking to disaster
Only much faster

Yet the spinning wheel sill goes round
And the people still go round
With their heads towards the ground

Heading for disaster
Only much faster

And although they have lengthened your life
You’ll be lucky if you survive the strife
Of the mid-life crisis

Heading for disaster
Only much faster

There’s just no time to stop and stare
“Hey you, what you doing down there?
You should be **doing** something, it’s not fair

Heading for disaster
Only much faster

“But I just wanted to stop and stare!”
“That so? - well it don’t get you anywhere

You should be **going** somewhere!"

Heading for disaster
Only much faster

An excerpt from married life

The day the builders came
It happened to be raining too
The day the builders came
My husband dropped his razor down the loo
We had to fish it out and
Clean it in disinfectant
It became, once again
Sparkling and new

The day the builders came
I was trying to write
But I couldn't type at all
Such a banging on the walls
I thought they were going to fall down

The day builders came
My mother invited herself to stay
But how could I say, please go away?
Such filial ingratitude would never do
And she had contributed quite considerably
To the cost of the extension too.

The day the builders came
I envisaged Utopia
Within a week or two
A blue bath, basin and loo
Central heating automatic
Through and through
Low windows with a view

Of the budding rose garden

The day the builders finished
When was that? Did they ever I wonder
The roses had all withered
The cold was not still seeping in
It had set in

We were all bedded by the flu
my mother too
She came again in Autumn rain
Her pink-petalled hat
Moist enough to make scent

The bathroom dream, was somehow green
The low windows were too low
And through our bones the wind did blow
The day the builders went though
Was yet still heaven sent
So we took the cotton wool from our ears
The silence was like sound in arrears
So were the bills, they remain unpaid
The garage was still full of bricks
So my husband took the bus to work instead

Storm

Storm
Electric
Storm
Electric
Thunder
And
Lightening
Rolling
Under
And
Frightening
Birds
Skies
Darkening
And
Lightening
My moods
Gather
As
The storm
Breaks
WAR
Shakes
The surface
Of the globe
The Gods revenge
Is
Storms
At sea
Storms
On land
Storms
Breaking
OUT
In
My

Consciousness
STOP
WARS
STOP
Anti-war marchers
Gather
Under
Their umbrellas
Receivers
Of SHOCK
Papers
Print
The HOLOCAUST
The Full Moon

Absorbs

The storms
Aftermath
The Lavender
Flowers
Suddenly
The lilacs sparkle
The daisies scream
On the lawn

Agony

Before

Being
Cut
Martyrs
Die
In
The storm
Trees fall
Down
The Gods
Revenge

For
The Holocaust
Before the Holocaust
Fight
And

I shall

Send
A PLAGUE OF
LOCUSTS

On you

My
Storm
Will
Wait
For
No
Tide
And
No wind
It starts
In
The minds
And
Consciousnesses
Of those
Who sinned

<u>Winter</u>

I meditate a lot in winter
I meditate upon a heater
If anybody thinks I'm cheating

Power of mind produces central heating

I find the concept of a fire
Increases my spirits so much higher
Than Krishna and the Holy Choir
Can ever do

I understand the problems of the nation
When it affects my circulation
Oppression of the working people
Who haven't got a chance to keep warm

It's not the one to make a fuss
But when it affects my arthritis
I'm afraid I have to scream and curse

I always wanted to be an Eskimo
Well, here's my chance to have a go
Here I am, alone and blue, in my igloo

As ice creeps up my window pane
I dream of summer country lanes
As snowman try to sleep with me
I clasp my hot water bottle to me

II

TOKYO

WAKES UP

Clouds

(Composed on the China airways flight to Japan, on my first Buddhist journey as a member of Soka Gakkai, April 1987)

Mountains in the sky
Lunar landing bases for UFOs
They are watching us!
Are we their foes?
Who knows?

From what distant star
Or nearer Moon or Mars
Can Islands in the sky
Leave such faint scars?
Of platforms, citadels and piers
Pinnacles and mosque-like souvenirs
Transported here
Outlines of distant habitations
Transported here

All jumble and mix
And atop a platform a Buddha sits
And then a wise old man
The seer of the earth
His beard so long
The ozone layer his girth
He sees pollution rise, and sighs
He sees the sun
That will soon radiate to man
A painful message
And the poles apart melting
And the rains that will fall soon
And the coming hurricane
The unexpected typhoon

That negativity the moon
Is cloudlike too
And every time the plane speeds forward
The moon moves too

This mirror land all topsy-turvy
These islands in the sky
The shadow of humanity
Divided by a line of infinity

And here and there
Like or Tweedledum and Tweedledee
By mirror landscapes
We are joined to we

On a third plane
Our images reflected in the sea
Clouds our astral souls
Life's shadows and our ghouls
And on platforms land the UFOs
Then descend by magnetic bends
To power points below
Knitted into the warp and weft of the world we know
By some unknown channel of energy, they arrive
Via clouds, to us below
To conduct their experiments
Are we friend or foe?
We hope to know what we do not know , Though:
I think they wish to help us down below

Poem - on Fallen Leaves (a view from the train on the Chuo Sen(Central Line, Tokyo

A frozen palm tree
Under a lemon sun
Frost on the fields.

A frozen persimmon.

The firs of Switzerland
The maples of USA,
The Autumn leaves of England
And Kyushu Tropicana
To take your breath away.

Gold glints on the Express Train.
Fortune's to be made
With early morning pain.
The apartment blocks and bars,
Harbour memories of wars.
The corrugated iron roofs
Hold shadows which remain.
A cemetery for the dead.
Bicycles in a bicycle shed.

Right now
Thousands of Japanese
Are awakening
In frozen scenes,
Next to railway lines.
Breathing dry air.
Crawling out of futons
Onto frozen tatami
Steam heaters on
To take away the pain
Up we get in early morning
All together
And pile onto the train.

Leaves of Autumn
What haven't we done this year?
Time's passing by.
Time to turn over a new leaf.
Comic leaves of manga,
Pages of insignificance.

Can they too
Not be thrown away,
Amongst the red leaves
Of a winter's day.

If, houses were gardens;
If flats were fields;
If parking lots were parks;
Then Autumn might be more beautiful.
Will I wake up in winter
And discover
This sheer beauty
Was nothing but a dream
The people packs of cards
On a desolate scene.
Packed together like sardines,
Are we real?
What hidden life
Was the man's
Who in alienation
Jumped onto the line
Between Takao and Shinjuku?

(Shorter version previously published in, 'The Light of the World'' The International Library of Poetry, 1997)

Tama River - 8.40am

So far from home
And yet so near the Humber
The Tama River meanders by
Under a grey and smoky sky
Factories spume out sulphurous smoke
Along the banks
Fumes of coke
People cough and choke
In the dry winter

And I, a poet,
Sit on the bank and consider
Yorkshire here
Same factories, same skies
Today, same damp rain
Black desolate scenes
Of Brönte country
And Ted Hughes landscape
Scarsdale Crag
Appears on the ragged river bank
Bleak winter trees
Line the river
The long, bleached grasses and bushes
Of Spurn Head appear
A jogger in red
Goes by

I have escaped
From the people and the trains
The cold, the heat, the cold again
Of early morning pain
Here, no people,
Only ravens and crows
Mourn the economic dream
Harbingers of desolation

Behind the fir trees of Switzerland
And blocks of flats
Mount Fuji stands majestic
Now hidden by the mists
Of a thousand factories
The skies have become
Cancerous
Our smoke filled
Ozone destroying environment

I am a poet
But I am afraid

This beautiful world
Was not made
To be destroyed by man
We should preserve nature's balance
If we can

No use
To cram us all together
In apartment blocks and trains
No point in running from A to B
Then back again

Forever going round and round
For what gain?
Look at the river
Not a soul in sight
A few ducks swim by
Oblivious of the world's storm
Their lives are simple and clean
Ours are so complicated and mean
Why do we live this lie?
Why not turn our eyes to the sky
And find the truth waiting
And realize our world is passing by
We have to save and nurture it
Before it is too late
Oh, Tama river, please wait
For man to make a better landscape.

Tokyo, Dec
1988

No More Waribashi (Disposable chopsticks)

No more waribashi
Every one's a tree
No more waribashi, for me.
No more waribashi
Don't be so greedy
In this throwaway society.

We live in the jungle
We ain't primitive you see.
We live in the jungle,
We're free.
We live in the jungle
We respect each living tree.
A forest is a university.

I've got a pair of chopsticks
I've had them all my life
I live in this village
With my wife.

My grandmother gave them to me
When I was only this high.
She said: These chopsticks
Will last you 'til you die.

In the 21st century
Rich nations gotta lot of money
But will they give any
To my family?

In the 21st Century
Rich nations gotta lot of money
But privilege entails responsibility.

If chopsticks are disposable
The question it is posable

How long before man is disposable too?

If chopsticks are disposable
The question it is posable
Are they going to
Throwaway the truth?

Kyo kara	From today
Watashi wa	I am
Restaurant	
Ni ikutoki wa,	When I go to the
restaurant	
Kyo kara	From today
Watashi wa	I am
Watashi no hashi motteimas	Bringing my non-
disposable chopsticks	
	With me
Waribashi dame	Waribashi are no
good	
Waribashi ki des	Waribashi are trees
Waribashi zenbu ki des	Waribashi are all
trees	
Waribashi dame	Waribashi are no
good	
Waribashi ki des	Waribashi are trees
Waribashi zenbu ki des.	Waribashi are all
trees.	

No more waribashi
Every one's a tree
No more waribashi for me
No more waribashi
Don't be so greedy
In this throwaway society.

(Japan wastes a lot of trees in making disposable chopsticks, which are mad of non-varnished wood and only used once. The point being that you can buy non-disposable ones which are made of varnished wood, bone or plastic and can be re-used.)

The Moment is Now

There is no past
There is no future
The moment is now!

Make your decision
Act with precision
Use not your mind
But your intuition

Do you feel it's right?
What does your heart tell you!
Act right now
Create your future
By your present moment.

Give yourself a new name!
You can do anything
Be anybody
You are the creator
And the creature
Of your reality!

(Previously published in Verse and Verbosity, by Poetry Today, 1998)

20th Century Rap to Freedom

You think you've got the vote; that's hip!
But you don't control one bit of it,
And what I fail to understand,
Is why 10% of Them, own the land.

And listen to the voice of bards,
Do not accept identity cards,
It's a dog's life - all that trip,
And the way to lose your citizenship.

Some smart guy with a smart card says:
'Accept world government to send your days.'
Single currency, single unity.
Not United Nations, but autocracy.

Before they came for us, we spoke:
'It's time for things to change, we're hoping;
Without some change we cannot cope,
But our identities shatter, are broken.'

Socrates was right; he had insight,
And now we need to speak our plight,
And be as brave as folks like he,
Who stood right up to tyranny.

The Socratic tradition can set us free.
Dialogue, it is the key;
To destroy the power of authority;
It can only happen between you and me.

You've got the power deep in you
To create the life that's true for you,
So create the future now, anew;
And aim to make your dream come true!
As the wise Socrates knew,
Nothing is better than freedom; true!

(Previously published in 'For Now and Forever', Poetry Today, 1999)

Reg – A Hale Vessel at the Age of Eighty (In port, Hull)

My name is Reg
I'm a sailor boy
Every kind of yacht
Is my favourite toy
I live out of suitcases
And like to travel
Across the Seven Seas
Many mysteries I've unravelled
My arm is long
And widely reaches
From the cold North country
To the Australian beaches
Everywhere I go my banner is unfurled
In countless places across the world
To those who suffer – I give hope
And counselling to those who mope
I'm everyone's friend
And dearly loved
I have time to spend
On those who are troubled
My countenance at eighty
Is like that of a youth
My eyes are bright
And my voice speaks the truth
I've great humanity
And lots of friends
To whom my words of wisdom
Helps to make amends
I take great pity
On some strange and odd relations
Who are mostly round the bend
And cause lots of consternations
I've got some odd cousins
And eccentric ancestors
But on the whole
I don't let family grudges fester

I like to party
With folk of all ages
I've got tales and jokes to tell
That many find outrageous
A seasoned sailor of life
At the age of 80
I can paint, draw, write –
And still look 20
I'm pretty fit and rather sporty
I don't like folk who are at all haughty
I live near one
I'd rather not mention
A deputy PM who failed
Due to naughty intentions
I don't like left or right
I'm in the middle
A conservative with a small c
I don't like riddles
Many folk come
And many folk go
To me they are all equal
They just need to learn to row
As I steer them on the right path
I'm really a Buddha
Though I don't chant at all
I help them steer their rudder
Be aware of sharks –
Is my legacy to all
When something's fishy I can smell it
But I sail round it – that's all
Crossing the line
Is my greatest triumph
So I'll have to go past 100
To realise my zenith
I'm a sailor of life
And I've won many battles
Across the Seven Seas
Successfully I've travelled

Mainly I'm a teacher
A teacher of life
Who is just like a ship
That has to be sailed right
Sometimes vessels go down
But they can come up again
They just need a bit of encouragement
From a sailor and a friend.
When I was younger
I blew smoke rings through a dimple
On my chin
And children wondered
If I was really a magician
Now I've triumphed on the high seas
The high seas of life
I'm ready to go on
Sailing on the ocean
And bringing out the sun.
With Yvonne, my darling wife.

An 80th birthday tribute to my cousin, April 2007

II

The

Reality

Of

Concrete Dreams

Fields of Europe

Idyllic fields are few and far between,
Becoming illusions of an urban dream.
The motorways ride roughshod over
The Downs, from London to Dover.
Protesters say: 'The motorway has had its day!',
But most people would rather ride the flyover,
Than walk the ramblers' path;
Would rather view nature in 3D,
On the cinema screen or on TV;
Than experience its power in calamity.
But nature is pure, wild, untamed.
It cannot be claimed on a TV screen,
Or netted on the internet;
Scrolled, or controlled by a computer.

Nature cannot be contained
In a European theme park,
So we can harp back to the times
When nature was free.
The people that sit on boards,
Sometimes forget that nature
Is more powerful than they.
Yet when the thunder hit's the roof, it says:
'You're not as powerful as me, I can easily
Tear down your Tower of Babylon,
Your electric chameleon!'
When the lines are down,
Those in Brussels may frown;
The Beast of Authority: Computer 666,
Has blown a circuit, and eaten its own chips!

(Previously published in As Life Goes By, Poetry Today, 2000)

Eternal Now

A THOUGHT

They make theme parks
Of things that are the past
Of things that are to come
But what about the eternal now?

They build to contain
Up to the sky
The internet
Our tool
To communicate by

A PROPHECY

And does the ugly Beast of 666
Fixed in Brussels
One currency, stamped, sealed and delivered
Rear its head?
Are all the heads of Europe on the level?
Or, are they all above board?
Are they Masonic Mafiosos
Fixing a conspiracy
To have us married, organized, not free?
All to be born with an identikit identity
Computer-chip-female, No 33
The young, trained on ecstasy
To abandon hope
Dope, to keep them fairly congenial and acquiescent
Not rude
Never honest, always crude

A COMMENT

We fight, we play

We relax in artificial pools
Under plastic palm trees
We entertain as fools
We see all the gardens of Europe
In a 3D show
But where did all the real gardens go?
They went, a long time ago.
Feel the simulated waves,
But, oh, I wish
The cool sea breeze to blow
I long for fish and chips by the pier
The real sands
And the Italian Gondolier
Did Socrates forsake us here -
On Italy's further shores?
Where are the real people?
Are they all replicas in a museum?
Or have they been cloned
And simply appear to be who they're not?
We can all type the hype to communicate
We can all talk to our dogs in the park
We do talk to our acquaintances on mobile phones
Anything o keep a distance
And true dialogue at bay
We can even talk to ourselves - nobody minds
They're all mad anyway
I'm an outsider, I always do
Talk to myself too
I create interest on the tube.

AN ASIDE

Maybe I'm mad
Does someone know?
I'm forty one
Alone in the cold
Who cares
If my dreams happen or not

Do you?
Do you care for your own dreams too?
Where are they?
Fight for them-
Don't you want to be whole.

A CONCLUSION

In this Tower of Babylon
This electric chameleon
Soon to be consumed
To become Atlantis, exhumed
For later generations to say:
The 20th century had its day
It went under!
Like civilizations did before
And though we came from the stars
The survivors are now back, living on Mars
Just a few crew of an escaped space-shop Ark
They saw the sphinx in Egypt on the red planet
They eyes were familiar
Like the Mona Lisa
They seemed to say:
There's room up here to start anew;
But what you're doing's nothing new!
They say, didn't this happen before
Perhaps on some other star?
Does not some faint memory glow
With history repeating itself

A SOLUTION

Now you know
We're trapped in a time warp
Trapped in a time warp
Trapped in a time warp, until we grow
Larger than our lesser selves
We'll keep on repeating our errors

Until we learn there's something better
And the time is NOW
To change dimensions
To move a chord up the scale of humanity
To operate from love
Not little ego, me
To recognize our higher selves
Either we win our place on a plain
Or we go under, and down again
And at the risk of repeating myself -
The time is now!

Some time in the 90's

Nostalgia

There used to be something called 'Society'
Now there's only cars.
People used to talk to each other;
Now they discuss life on Mars
With their dogs. Or talk; unsociably;
To work colleagues far away;
On their mobile phones, in bars.

There used to be something called the NHS.
Now it seems they couldn't care less.
And if you want new teeth; it's like getting a new car.
They tell you, you have to pay for them.
White fillings for those who can pay.
Metal fillings for those on low or no pay.
And if you get nervous about injections,
There's a place in Hackney they can send you away;
To where you can be put out for the day.

Soon, the over sixties may have to pay
For exit visas to those Pearly Gates;

And those who pass the Euthanasia laws,
Remain unaware of the cause
To murder they make, by taking life away.
Now wisdom's out; is Solyent Green on the way?*

In the Autumn there used to be leaves.
Now there's only litter; urban sleaze.
The legacy's bitter - choking trees.

Now doctors can strike us off their lists
If they don't like us; am I likely to be missed?
Was my life a poem; an art of struggle?
Or did I do nothing; just kept out of trouble.

* Solyent Green was a film set in a futuristic America in which old people volunteered for euthanasia and were then turned into green protein biscuits (without their knowledge), which were then fed back to the general population, as food supplies dwindled.

(Previously published in Reach for the Truth, Poetry Today, 1999

Black Lady of the Caribbean

Who acknowledged her?
Where is her statue?
Who named her after English towns,
Put her to work in fields, and beat her?
Black lady of the Caribbean;
An unpaid slave of the Empire,
Never credited for years of service.
She represents all and none of Africa;
Because she was uprooted
From her place of birth,
And sent in chains to work
From dawn 'til dusk, in plantations.

Abused and used by her owners,
Sometimes she gained a Scottish, Chinese, Irish name
And bore children against her will.
When she came to the West
Hollywood cast her in the role of nanny, 'mammy', maid,
Comforter and carer of the white woman.
She did this for years too,
Before being given the right to vote.
Then she was put to work as a cleaner,
In the hospitals, in old people's homes;
Caring for those nobody cared for.
Did she not teach us endurance, compassion and charity,
Despite what we did to her?
By her example, she forgave us, with a big heart;
Have we ever respected her,
For all her years of service?
Let's raise her statue high above the Thames in Gold
With the inscription: 'I made it!' - Such is her story told.

(Previously published in Poets Around London and Home Counties 2000), Poetry Today, 2000

The Brockley Mums

The Brockley mums, go out with prams,
Their babies big and beaming
They have big bums and big fat tums
And they're usually weaning.

In twos and threes they pram around,
Their feet placed firmly on the ground
In jeans and 70s flowery tops,
Or 100% cotton summer frocks,
Occasionally sporting socks.

They meet in vegetarian 'cafés'
And gladly swallow back a quaff
Of organic wine with a rocket lunch,
While baby eats an organic munch.

Baby's nappies are all biodegradable,
Made of brown recycled paper
They're usually quite cheerful and cheeky
And sometimes just a little leaky.

They have Victorian houses in Hilly Fields,
From which they walk in their flat heels
Hubby, he is always out,
While Mum jut has to pram about.

Their husbands are freelance and arty,
The mums have a lot of baby parties
Oh what a nice life they don't work,
While folk like me leave theirs in a nursery.

(Previously published in Mixed Emotions, United Press, 2005)

Poem on a London Bus

I've really had enough
Of this bus.
The shouting, the bumping, the obscenities
And all that stuff.
It's a blight in the world of buses –
A big mistake.
The only trouble is –
It gets me to work – late.
But I have no other choice.
I am a passenger without a voice.
And even if I yell at drivers, inspectors and all.

They never give an honest answer to my call.

I am forced to sit next to whales
Who think that the seat is for two, at least.
Or men with no manners, legs apart.
I feel like jerking them back into place with spanners.

Don't people know a seat
Is for one, not two;
Then they expect me to squash into the corner too,
So they can have most of my seat!
What a cheat!

Then there's the pram pushers,
Who always decide to travel at rush hours
And block the bus so no one can get past.
Or the chewing gum poppers
Who won't shut up
When everybody sighs.

Yes, I've really had enough of this bus.
Four years of hell.
And now I analyse each person who gets on
With one thing in mind:
How wide is their butt?
Can the seat next to me accommodate them or not?
If not, I place my briefcase on the seat,
So in this case
I won't give them the space.
If they complain,
I glare at them
Until they go away.
Selfish or not,
I've had a lot to put up with,
Now they're getting it back.

So I became selfish to protect my space
So I can sit on my seat

Without being pushed off my feet.

I gather, the government would like us to
Leave our cars at home
And rely on public transport to
Get us to where we want to go
But don't they know
Buses don't know their own timetable,
And come and go as they please -
And I have on occasions, been asked
To direct new drivers along the route.
Buses also like to get from A to B
As quickly as possible, without stopping,
Sometimes following each other in threes,
Not thinking much about picking up you and me.
WHAT IS A BUS FOR??
I've asked myself this a thousand times or more.
Is a bus for us –
Or against us?
Yes, I've really, really, really
Had enough of this bus.

2003

The Fig Tree

Early evening
And the sound of children playing,
Drums beating rap.
A happy sound of early summer
Hints of a fairground,
Modern, the present, now.
The fig tree,
On the other hand,
Has many pasts,
Knows many secrets.

Is magnificence, in the middle of the courtyard,
Protects us from the cars.
Its leaves like open palms, with fat, green fingers.
It's a benefactor,
Over spilling its fruit,
Occasionally near our heads.
It's crying teardrop shaped figs,
That nobody picks up and eats,
Being not quite ripe and rather rubbery.
Maybe it would wish to be
In a Mediterranean land.
It gives us shelter from the heat,
Links arms with ivy
To form a retreat
Its fruit smells faintly scented and jammy
It's a figure of abundance
For us.
When the wind rustles its leaves it's saying:
"Throw my secrets to the breeze
Of coaches, horses, ladies and gentlemen,
Children playing and family parties.
It's seen plagues, famine, fire, diseases,
Death, mirth and rebirth."
Others have come and gone but
Its still here,
It just grows bigger,
Year by year.
The fig tree
Is a symbol of continuity
In the 21st century.

(Written while teaching a creative writing class in Summer 2002,. I asked the students to write a poem on the fig tree in the courtyard, while we all sat out one afternoon.)

<u>Iraq</u>

Oh Mesopotamia
Your country weeps.

Your people, trampled underfoot;
The birthplace of Abraham, Ur, defiled.
What was once the original Garden of Eden,
In the North,
Is now a place of frozen plums, never plucked
And suspended in time.
In the South
Now poisoned by chemicals;
The desert blows its deadly wind
Tainted with Uranium dust,
Into all corners.

Families weep.
Malnourished 'sugar babies',
Fed on tea and water,
Their mothers unable to produce milk
Or only tainted milk
After years of sanctions;
Explode and die
In their mothers' arms.
Homes without furniture,
Sold for food.
A house displays an old, faded picture
Of Bobby Charlton,
Pinned on the wall,
Flapping in the breeze.
The family said:
'We like English football.'
Yet, I am ashamed to say,
England helped to perpetuate this crisis.

The Iraqi National Orchestra
Plays on with dignity, without strings,
Like the one on the last days of the Titanic.
The music, proud and dignified,
Drowns us with sorrow.
Strings were banned,
In case they could be made into weapons.

No morphine in the hospitals;
People die.
A genocide of future generations,
Wiped out for nothing.

Why should the most fertile country in the world
Be destroyed,
Its sons sent to fight,
Its daughters without husbands,
Its children without food?

The Moloch worshippers,
With their pagan rites
Are Greedy for oil
And ready to sacrifice more children in war,
Hypocritically, they worship that
Which came from Babylon,
Yet plan to destroy that city today.
A country with oil is cursed
If it produces no wealth for its own citizens,
But is fought over by those who fear
Their resources and profits are running low.

Infiltrators from all sides
Creep into Iraq's borders;
Assassins, rebels, black marketeers,
New and greedy politicians and parties,
Incited to destroy the old
Without anything new that's better,
Backed by those with their eyes on oil,
Oil and more oil.
What use is oil
If a people can't eat?

Politicians talk of weapons,
Both chemical and biological,
But who manufactured and sold them originally?

Who are the guilty ones?
Who would like to make more money
From selling more weapons?
Human Greed is guilty –
And he's a big sinner
And cuts across all boundaries and nations,
But some might be guiltier than others.

The origins of civilisation
Echo through Iraq,
The seat of learning, science, maths
And erudition started here.
Now her children have no books in schools
Or even no schools,
Except a bombed out skeleton of a school;
Growing up illiterate, waiting for the next war.
What is this world I was born into?
Where the strong, with their talons,
Swoop down in the night
And prey on the weak.
Care has been cruelly cremated;
Hear the children's cries,
See the burning bodies,
Cities going up in flames.
Are we not ashamed?

Jan 2003

<u>Saddam</u>

Saddam
A sad man.
Once so great, so revered, so feared.
Now hanging from a noose.
Did he think that he would end up this way?
Did he really think they would do away
With him in this manner?

Some say,
It's not really him
Some other double is
Paying for his sins.
The teeth don't match
Those in the charming grins
When he was in power.
Who knows?
Are we supposed to know?
Anyway a man died
And he showed courage
And recited his Koran
Whatever he did, he did,
But his passing was jeered by some
And mourned by others.
So we are barbarians after all
That we allowed ourselves
No decent condemnation
By allowing others
To act like terrorists by taunting
The accused
As if our leaders
Were some kind of angels
Who can be excused
Of bombing the innocent
And sending many young men
To certain death
Saddam
A sad man
Is no more Jan
2007

Signs of the Times - Defective Line

How many engineers
Does it take, to repair a line?
One to repair it; ten to supervise him;
And twenty to manage them.

A defective train line;
In the rain,
We are all in pain.
Leaving work again, on time;
Tonight, I wanted
An early night.
Someone says,
The new tracks are moulded,
So they take longer to repair.
(Some idiot must have decided
That made
life simpler!)

No apologies, no explanations;
As we trundle back and forth past stations.
No free cups of tea.
We might even see
The apple core, thrown out the window,
Turn into a tree.
Whoever's got supplies of food and drink,
On the crowded, rush hour train,
Is to be envied, as the wait drives us insane.

Very sneakily, they do not tell us,
We're going across the river - twice.
They park the train high on a bridge
Over Waterloo.
We cannot get out,
Or even to the loo.
There's too many people to push through.

However, one could
Smash the window,
And jump onto
A doubler decker bus,
Way down below,
If, one wanted to.

We departed from Charing Cross,
We're now at Cannon Street.
They won't open the door,
Until a woman shouts - (me incidentally),
I wanna get out!
I wanna cup of tea!
The doors open, immediately.

Oh, Englanders, be fools no more!
The time is ripe for revolution on our shore!
We are too tolerant; we've been had again,
No one fights back, we just complain.
Negative values, make us inane.

I want a refund, AND
A cup of tea!
I feel like shouting
At no one particularly.
We get angry inside,
Always being taken for a ride,
That leads us nowhere.

Why are we always the last train to leave,
Metaphorically?
Do the English like to wait,
Until it is too late,
Just to be on the safe side?
The Japanese have trains
That go always, and all ways;
Up and down, magnetic and
All around the town.

They know performance; pays.

But we, the English,
Frown upon what's new.
We prefer the old, the borrowed,
And the truly blue.
Though it often gets us into a stew,
Because it's slow and inefficient too.

It seems we're back at Waterloo.
Here I change my train three times.
Lucky for some, but not for me;
The third train, for Hayes, though in more early;
For some strange reason is leaving rather late.
It departs when we are all irate
With sighs, rustles, tuts and frowns.
Dinners are waiting out of town.

In Ladywell, the rain is pouring down.
It's eight o'clock instead
Of six.
The only man who apologizes is,
The railway counter clerk;
Who's packing up to go.
'Sorry', he says.
'We apologize for the delay.
I hope it didn't spoil your day!'
He takes responsibility for all those who
Didn't on the way.
'You're the only one who's said, "Sorry" today',
I say.

Concrete Brains

People who live in concrete
Have social problems
Something about the concrete
Makes them weak.
With concrete brains
They are full of pain.
Concrete; leaking water
Drawing in the whistling wind.
Cold from up
And between the windows
The wind blows
Over trashed balconies
Laden with junk
Defiled by pigeons
Looking for crumbs
And a safe corner
To rest and breed.
Concrete screams
Swear words.
People and dogs
Leave their mark
In the elevator;
Going up and down
Creaking,
People frown
'I don't know how they get in
They think it's just as dustbin
And we live here;
They don't have a key
They follow you and me,
Lumbering in
With a can of drink;
And, oh my God,
They don't half stink!'

I believe
Everyone in England has access to running water
Even if it's in the fountain in Trafalgar.

<u>Promises of Pyramids</u>

The Council Brotherhood
Are at it again
They like to build misshapen stone pyramids
In the middle of roundabouts
Or put up obelisks on The Green
To consolidate the vortices
Of male power
But do they care about the rats. the drains, the leaks, the floods, the overflows
From aging tower blocks? - No!
They like to spend their money
On useless projects
Created merely to fill
In their time
And delay ours
They love giving out
Bits of paper
Coffee, sandwiches, free pens, working papers
Information packs with no information in
But as far as doing anything
They do not *do*
They merely plan and think and talk, talk, talk
'Let's discuss the options', they say
'Think about it for a day
Or two
Before we tell you'
Then they go away
They have something more important to do
Like a Council Meeting

Or an overseas trip
To Italy or the South of France
Where they can meet, eat, talk and dance
With other council strays from far away
Who are also fully funded and
Fully fattened by the end of their break
They are really cheating everyone around
A year or two later
We are no wiser
As to the options
Gossip is going around
They're going to pull us down
Someone took a backhander
And they changed their tune
They're going to send us out of town
Rebuild, redevelop
All they promise is a lot of codswallop!
Pull down the blocks
Get rid of the have nots
And build some new eco friendly flats
Only for key workers. (Oct 04,
reworked, Jan 08)

<u>Expansion</u> (To Ashford, Kent)

Expansion relentlessly
Claws back sheep.
To whit! To whoo!
Moloch's building
A new D.I.Y. too;
Spreads its warehouse wings
Over terraces
Preying on the unsuspecting poorer, middle classes.
'We want your plot!' screeches the guy at the top
Just think what a lot
Of houses we could build
If we got rid of YOU!
At least two in your garden

And possibly a dual carriageway or two.

Everyone should come and live here, they say,
Except you lot in Victorian houses, GO AWAY!
And take your bowling clubs, businesses
And allotments with you.
We need fresh blood to slave in retail stores
And bars for rail and car passengers.

Don't think you can relax
Our eyes are everywhere, beware.
Eyes that gleam and stare,
Obsessed with greed and profit.
We banish care.
The master plan is masterful,
As the grand architects and planners
Plot their way through OUR town
Then retire to their villages.

Their talons tear into our souls
Their eyebrows frown expansively
With lack of vision or wisdom.

They have no respect for our lives,
Yet they think they can buy us off with cash.

Empty Poets

On the TV
Empty poets
They know it
We know it, too
We are not in the know
We are the culture below
We cannot create
Cannot be full people
We are just watchers, waiters, collectors

Traitors to culture
Which is so highbrow
We cannot know how to think
We cannot link in
Yet obtain no benefit by dreaming.

Let's be plotters instead
Screaming to create the poetry of life
Street poets
Poets of life
Poets of work
Listen to our cries over the rooftops
Art critics try to tell us
What they'd like us to know
But we all know
Real art
Comes from the heart
It's not a show!

(Empty poets was inspired after watching a rather highbrow arts show on the TV, where I felt poetry was being portrayed as a dead fiction, only accessible to those in tough with 'high culture'. I would say poetry is about life, something which is created and inspired by one's heart. Everyone has unlimited potential and creativity which they can develop to create art. It's a matter of finding the key to do this. For me, the key has been my Buddhist practice. I was most surprised to receive a book prize for submitting this poem to Voices, where it was previously published by Poetry Today in 1996)

NAM-MYOHO-RENGE-KYO

Chant for peace!

Printed in the United Kingdom by
Lightning Source UK Ltd., Milton Keynes
138182UK00002B/63/P

9 781849 234245